SEEKERS

TOKLO'S STORY

Seekers: Toklo's Story
Created by Erin Hunter
Written by Dan Jolley
Art by Bettina M. Kurkoski

Lettering - John Hunt
Production Artist - Michael Paolilli
Graphic Designer - Chelsea Windlinger

Editor - Lillian Diaz-Przybyl
Print Production Manager - Lucas Rivera
Managing Editor - Vy Nguyen
Senior Designer - Louis Csontos
Director of Sales and Manufacturing - Allyson De Simone
Associate Publisher - Marco F. Pavia
President and C.O.O. - John Parker
C.E.O. and Chief Creative Officer - Stu Levy

A Manga

TOKYOPOP and 🐢 are trademarks or registered trademarks of TOKYOPOP Inc.

TOKYOPOP Inc.
5900 Wilshire Blvd. Suite 2000
Los Angeles, CA 90036

E-mail: info@TOKYOPOP.com
Come visit us online at www.TOKYOPOP.com

For information address HarperCollins Children's Books, a division of HarperCollins Publishers,
10 East 53rd Street, New York, NY 10022.
www.harpercollinschildrens.com
ISBN 978-0-06-172380-3
Library of Congress catalog card number: 2009921415
12 13 14 LP/BV 10 9 8 7 6 5 4 3 2
❖
First Edition

SEEKERS

TOKLO'S STORY

CREATED BY
ERIN HUNTER

WRITTEN BY
DAN JOLLEY

ART BY
BETTINA M. KURKOSKI

HAMBURG // LONDON // LOS ANGELES // TOKYO

HARPER
An Imprint of HarperCollinsPublishers

THEN WE'LL
BE ABLE TO DO
ANYTHING WE WANT.

WAKE UP.

IT'S TIME TO GO.

HZZRRRH?

WHY DO WE HAVE TO LEAVE OUR CAVE EVERY DAY, MOM?

YOU KNOW WHY.

THAT BIG BROWN BEAR DOESN'T WANT US IN THIS PART OF THE FOREST.

I ALREADY HATE NOT HAVING OUR DEN.

IT WAS FUN AT FIRST--GOING OFF ON AN ADVENTURE LIKE THIS--BUT NOW IT'S GETTING COLD.

I STILL DON'T UNDERSTAND WHY MOM GOT SO MAD AT ME. SHE SAID A BUNCH OF THINGS THAT DIDN'T MAKE ANY SENSE.

BUT WE'RE ON THE MOVE AGAIN...AND EVEN THOUGH WE'RE TIRED AND HUNGRY, AT LEAST WHILE WE'RE MOVING WE'RE NOT SO COLD.

TOBI...

I'M OKAY! I CAN DO IT!

TOBI, HERE. GRAB ONTO MY TAIL. I'LL HELP YOU.

WE'VE ALWAYS LOVED PLAYING IN THE SNOW BEFORE. BUT THE SNOW'S NO FUN NOW.

ESPECIALLY WITH NO DEN TO GO BACK TO.

I SHOULD HAVE KNOWN! THAT ROCK WAS JUST STUCK IN THE ICE!

HANG ON, TOBI!

HEEELP! MAMAAAAA!

TOBI, SWIM! SWIM, I'LL GRAB YOU--!

WALKING ALONG NEXT TO TOBI...
FOR JUST A LITTLE WHILE I CAN
SORT OF FORGET THE MESS WE'RE IN.

IT'S EASY TO
PRETEND AGAIN.

TO BE THE KINGS OF
THE MOUNTAIN AGAIN.

WHOA... GOOD NOSE!

COME ON, TOBI! EAT UP!

BUT...WHAT IF THIS BELONGS TO THE BIG BEAR?

IT'S OKAY—HE LEFT IT HERE, DIDN'T HE? HE MUST HAVE CAUGHT SO MUCH FOOD, HE HAS LEFTOVERS!

BESIDES, YOU'RE THE ONE WHO FOUND IT!

I TEAR INTO THE DELICIOUS MEAT, BUT TOBI ONLY EATS A FEW MOUTHFULS...

...AND ALL OF A SUDDEN IT HITS ME!

HEY, WE SHOULD BE TAKING THIS BACK TO MOM!

OKAY!

I KNOW I HAVE TO DO SOMETHING. WE'RE IN THE BIG BEAR'S DEN--HE'S GOING TO FIND US. BUT WHILE I'M TRYING TO FIGURE OUT WHAT TO DO...

...TOBI DOES SOMETHING I DON'T EXPECT AT ALL.

I'M HERE.

ME.

MY NAME'S TOBI.

YOU AGAIN.

WHERE'S THE OTHER ONE? THERE WERE TWO OF YOU.

ERIN
HUNTER

is inspired by a fascination with
the ferocity of the natural world.
As well as having great respect for
nature in all its forms, Erin enjoys
creating rich mythical explanations
for animal behavior. She is also the
author of the Warriors series.

Visit Erin Hunter online at
www.warriorcats.com and
www.seekerbears.com.

For exclusive information on your
favorite authors and artists, visit
www.authortracker.com.

DON'T MISS THE SECOND
SEEKERS MANGA:

SEEKERS

KALLIK'S ADVENTURE

Polar bear cub Kallik and her brother, Taqqiq, live in a cozy den nestled into the side of a snowy hill. Their mother, Nisa, tells them endless stories of the outside world and Kallik and Taqqiq can't wait to explore everything. Nisa says they're too little to leave the den, but that won't stop them from sneaking out and having all sorts of thrilling adventures on their own!

TURN THE PAGE FOR A SNEAK PEEK AT

SEEKERS

THE QUEST BEGINS

SEEKERS

THE QUEST BEGINS

CHAPTER ONE

Kallik

"*A long, long time ago, long* before bears walked the earth, a frozen sea shattered into pieces, scattering tiny bits of ice across the darkness of the sky. Each of those pieces of ice contains the spirit of a bear, and if you are good, and brave, and strong, one day your spirit will join them."

Kallik leaned against her mother's hind leg, listening to the story she had heard so many times before. Beside her, her brother, Taqqiq, stretched, batting at the snowy walls of the den with his paws. He was always restless when the weather trapped them inside.

"When you look carefully at the sky," Kallik's mother continued, "you can see a pattern of stars in the shape of the Great Bear, Silaluk. She is running around and around the Pathway Star."

"Why is she running?" Kallik chipped in. She knew the answer, but this was the part of the story where she always asked.

"Because it is snow-sky and she is hunting. With her quick and powerful claws, she hunts seal and beluga whale. She is the greatest of all hunters on the ice."

Kallik loved hearing about Silaluk's strength.

"But then the ice melts," Nisa said in a hushed voice. "And she can't hunt anymore. She gets hungrier and hungrier, but she has to keep running because three hunters pursue her: Robin, Chickadee, and Moose Bird. They chase her for many moons, all through the warm days, until the end of burn-sky. Then, as the warmth begins to leave the earth, they finally catch up to her.

"They gather around her and strike the fatal blow with their spears. The heart's blood of the Great Bear falls to the ground, and everywhere it falls the leaves on the trees turn red and yellow. Some of the blood falls on Robin's chest, and that is why the bird has a red breast."

"Does the Great Bear die?" breathed Taqqiq.

"She does," Nisa replied. Kallik shivered. Every time she heard this story it frightened her all over again. Her mother went on.

"But then snow-sky returns, bringing back the ice. Silaluk is reborn and the ice-hunt begins all over again, season after season."

Kallik snuggled into her mother's soft white fur. The walls of the den curved up and around them, making a sheltering cave of snow that Kallik could barely glimpse in the dark, although it was only a few pawlengths from her nose. Outside a fierce wind howled across the ice, sending tendrils of freezing air through the entrance tunnel into their den. Kallik was glad they didn't have to be out there tonight.

Inside the den, she and her brother were warm and safe. Kallik wondered if Silaluk had ever had a mother and brother, or a den where she could hide from the storms. If the Great Bear had a family to keep her safe, maybe she wouldn't have to run from the hunters. Kallik knew her mother would protect her from anything scary until she was big enough and strong enough and smart enough to protect herself.

Taqqiq batted at Kallik's nose with his large furry paw. "Kallik's scared," he teased. She could make out his eyes gleaming in the darkness.

"Am not!" Kallik protested.

"She thinks robins and chickadees are going to come after her," Taqqiq said with an amused rumble.

"No, I don't!" Kallik growled, digging her claws into the snow. "That's not why I'm scared!"

"Ha! You *are* scared! I knew it!"

Nisa nudged Kallik gently with her muzzle. "Why are you frightened, little one? You've heard the legend of the Great Bear many times before."

"I know," Kallik said. "It's just . . . it reminds me that soon snow-sky will be over, and the snow and ice will all melt away.

And then we won't be able to hunt anymore, and we'll be hungry all the time. Right? Isn't that what happens during burn-sky?"

Kallik's mother sighed, her massive shoulders shifting under her snow-white pelt. "Oh, my little star," she murmured. "I didn't mean to worry you." She touched her black nose to Kallik's. "You haven't lived through a burn-sky yet, Kallik. It's not as terrible as it sounds. We'll find a way to survive, even if it means eating berries and grass for a little while."

"What is berries and grass?" Kallik asked.

Taqqiq wrinkled his muzzle. "Does it taste as good as seals?"

"No," Nisa said, "but berries and grass will keep you alive, which is the important thing. I'll show them to you when we reach land." She fell silent. For a few heartbeats, all Kallik could hear was the thin wail of the wind battering at the snowy walls.

She pressed closer to her mother, feeling the warmth radiating from her skin. "Are you sad?" she whispered.

Nisa touched Kallik with her muzzle again. "Don't be afraid," she said, a note of determination in her voice. "Remember the story of the Great Bear. No matter what happens, the ice will always return. And all the bears gather on the edge of the sea to meet it. Silaluk will always get back on her paws. She's a survivor, and so are we."

"I can survive anything!" Taqqiq boasted, puffing up his fur. "I'll fight a walrus! I'll swim across an ocean! I'll battle all the white bears we meet!"

"I'm sure you will, dear. But why don't you start by going to sleep?" Nisa suggested.

As Taqqiq circled and scuffled in the snow beside her, making himself comfortable, Kallik rested her chin on her mother's back and closed her eyes. Her mother was right; she didn't need to be afraid. As long as she was with her family, she'd always be safe and warm, like she was right now in their den.

Kallik woke to an eerie silence. Faint light filtered through the walls, casting pale blue and pink shadows on her mother and brother as they slept. At first she thought her ears must be full of snow, but when she shook her head, Nisa grunted in her sleep, and Kallik realized that it was quiet because the storm had finally passed.

"Hey," she said, poking her brother with her nose. "Hey, Taqqiq, wake up. The storm has stopped."

Taqqiq lifted his head with a bleary expression. The fur on one side of his muzzle was flattened, making him look lopsided.

Kallik barked with laughter. "Come on, you big, lazy seal," she said. "Let's go play outside."

"All right!" Taqqiq said, scrambling to his paws.

"Not without me watching you," their mother muttered with her eyes still closed. Kallik jumped. She'd thought Nisa was asleep.

"We won't go far," Kallik promised. "We'll stay right next to the den. Please can we go outside?"

Nisa huffed and the fur on her back quivered like a breeze was passing over it. "Let's all go out," she said. She pushed herself to her massive paws and turned around carefully in the small space, bundling her cubs to one side.

Sniffing cautiously, she nosed her way down the entrance tunnel, brushing away snow that the storm had piled up.

Kallik could see tension in her mother's hindquarters. "I don't know why she's so careful," she whispered to her brother. "Aren't white bears the biggest, scariest animals on the ice? Nothing would dare attack us!"

"Except maybe a bigger white bear, seal-brain!" Taqqiq retorted. "Maybe you haven't noticed how little you are."

Kallik bristled. "I may not be as big as you," she growled, "but I'm just as fierce!"

"Let's find out!" Taqqiq challenged as their mother finally padded out of the tunnel. He sprinted after her, sliding down the slope of the tunnel and scrambling out into the snow.

Kallik leaped to her paws and chased him. A clump of snow fell on her muzzle on her way out of the tunnel and she shook her head vigorously to get it off. The fresh, cold air tingled in her nostrils, full of the scent of fish and ice and faraway clouds. Kallik felt the last of her sleepiness melt away. The ice was where she belonged, not underground, buried alive. She batted a chunk of snow at Taqqiq, who dodged away with a yelp.

He chased her in a circle until she dove into the fresh snow, digging up clumps with her long claws and breathing in the sparkling whiteness. Nisa sat watching them, chuffing occasionally and sniffing the air with a wary expression.

"I'm coming for you," Taqqiq growled at Kallik, crouching low to the ground. "I'm a ferocious walrus, swimming through the water to get you." He pushed himself through the snow with his paws. Kallik braced herself to jump away, but before she could move, he leaped forward and bowled her over. They rolled through the snow, squalling excitedly, until Kallik managed to wriggle free.

"Ha!" she cried.

"Roar!" Taqqiq bellowed. "The walrus is really angry now!" He dug his paws into the snow, kicking a spray of white ice into their mother's face.

"Hey," Nisa growled. She cuffed Taqqiq lightly with her massive paw, knocking him to the ground. "That's enough snowballing around. It's time to find something to eat."

"Hooray, hooray!" Kallik yipped, jumping around her mother's legs. They hadn't eaten since before the storm, two sunrises ago, and her tummy was rumbling louder than Taqqiq's walrus roar.

The sun was hidden by trails of gray clouds that grew thicker as they walked across the ice, turning into rolls of fog that shrouded the world around them. The only sound Kallik could hear was the snow crunching under their paws. Once she thought she heard a bird calling from up in the sky, but when she looked up she couldn't see anything but drifting fog.

"Why is it so cloudy?" Taqqiq complained, stopping to rub his eyes with his paws.

"The fog is good for us," Nisa said, touching her nose to the ice. "It hides us as we hunt, so our prey won't see us coming."

"I like to see where I'm going," Taqqiq insisted. "I don't like walking in clouds. Everything's all blurry and wet."

"I don't mind the fog," Kallik said, breathing in the heavy, misty air.

"You can ride on my back," Nisa said to her son, nudging him with her muzzle. Taqqiq rumbled happily and scrambled up, clutching at tufts of her snow-white fur to give himself a boost. He stretched out on her back, high above Kallik, and they started walking again.

Kallik liked finding the sharp, cool scent of the ice under the dense, watery smell of the fog. She liked the hint of oceans and fish and salt and faraway sand that drifted through the scents, reminding her of what was below the ice and what it connected to. She glanced up at her mother, who had her nose lifted and was sniffing the air, too. Kallik knew that her mother wasn't just drawing in the crisp, icy smells. Nisa was studying them, searching for a clue that would lead them to food.

"You should both do this, too," Nisa said. "Try to find any smell that stands out from the ice and snow."

Taqqiq just snuggled farther into her fur, but Kallik tried to imitate her mother, swinging her head back and forth as she sniffed. She had to learn everything she could from Nisa so she could take care of herself. At least she still had a long time before that day came—all of burn-sky and the next snow-sky as well.

"Some bears can follow scents for skylengths," Nisa said. "All the way to the edge of the sky and then the next edge and the next."

Kallik wished her nose were that powerful. Maybe it would be one day.

Nisa lifted her head and started trotting faster. Taqqiq dug his claws in to stay on her back. Soon Kallik saw what her mother was heading for—a hole in the ice. She knew what that meant. *Seals!*

Nisa put her nose close to the ice and sniffed all around the edge of the hole. Kallik followed closely, sniffing everywhere her mother sniffed. She was sure she could smell a faint trace of seal. This must be one of the breathing holes where a seal would surface to take a breath before hiding down in the freezing water again.

"Seals are so dumb," Taqqiq observed from his perch on Nisa's back. "If they can't breathe in the water, why do they live in it? Why don't they live on land, like white bears?"

"Perhaps because then it'd be much easier for bears like us to catch them and eat them!" Kallik guessed.

"*Shhhh.* Concentrate," Nisa said. "Can you smell the seal?"

"I think so," Kallik said. It was a furry, blubbery smell, thicker than the smell of fish. It made her mouth water.

"All right," Nisa said, crouching by the hole. "Taqqiq, come down and lie next to your sister." Taqqiq obeyed, sliding off her back and padding over to Kallik. "Be very quiet," Nisa instructed them. "Don't move, and don't make a sound."

Kallik and Taqqiq did as she said. They had done this several times before, so they knew what to do. The first time, Taqqiq had gotten bored and started yawning and fidgeting. Nisa had cuffed him and scolded him, explaining that his noise would scare away the only food they'd seen in days. By now the cubs were both nearly as good at staying quiet as their mother was.

Kallik watched the breathing hole, her ears pricked and her nose keenly aware of every change in the air. A small wind blew drifts of snow across the ice, and the fog continued to roll around all three bears, making Kallik's fur feel wet and heavy.

After a while she began to get restless. She didn't know how her mother could stand to do nothing for such a long time, watching and watching in case the seal broke through the water. The chill of the ice below her was beginning to seep through Kallik's thick fur. She had to force herself not to shiver and send vibrations through the ice that might warn the seal they were there.

She stared past the tip of her nose at the ice around the breathing hole. The dark water below the surface lapped at the jagged edge. It was strange to think that that same dark water was only a muzzlelength below her, on the other side of the thick ice. The ice seemed so strong and solid, as if it went down forever. . . .

Strange shadows and shapes seemed to dance inside the ice, forming bubbles and whorls. It was odd—ice was white from far away but nearly clear up close and full of patterns. It almost seemed like things were living inside the ice. Right below her front paws, for instance, there was a large, dark bubble slowly moving from one side to the other. Kallik stared at it, wondering if it was the spirit of a white bear trapped in the ice. One that hadn't made it as far as the stars in the sky.

Taqqiq leaned over and peered at the bubble. "You know what Mother says," he whispered. "The shapes below the ice are dead bears. They're watching you . . . right . . . now."

"I'm not scared," Kallik insisted. "They're trapped inside the ice, aren't they? So they can't come out and hurt me."

"Not unless the ice melts," Taqqiq said, trying to sound menacing.

"Hush," Nisa growled, her eyes still fixed on the breathing hole. Taqqiq fell silent again, resting his head on his paws. Slowly his eyes began to droop, and soon he was asleep.

Kallik was feeling sleepy, too, but she wanted to stay awake to see the seal come out. And she didn't want to fall asleep so close to the spirit that was still moving below her feet. She flexed her paws, trying not to nod off.

Suddenly there was a splash, and Kallik saw a sleek gray head break through the surface of the water. She barely had time to notice the dark spots on its fur before Nisa was lunging headfirst into the hole. With a swift movement, she seized the seal and flipped it out of the water onto the ice. It writhed and flopped for a moment before her giant claw sliced into it, killing it with a single blow.

Kallik couldn't imagine ever being fast enough to catch a seal before it disappeared back under the ice again.

Nisa ripped open the seal and said the words of thanks to the ice spirits. Her cubs gathered around her to feed. Kallik inhaled the smell of freshly killed meat, the delicious fat and chewy skin. She dug her teeth into the prey and tore out a mouthful, realizing how hungry she had been.

Suddenly Nisa raised her head, her fur bristling. Kallik tensed and sniffed the air. A large male white bear was lumbering out of the fog toward them. His yellowish fur was matted with snow and his paws were as big as Kallik's head. He headed straight for their seal, hissing and rumbling.

Taqqiq bristled, but Nisa shoved him back with her paw. "Stay close to me," she warned. "Let's get out of here."

She turned to run, nudging her cubs ahead of her. Kallik sprinted as fast as she could, her heart pounding. What if the seal wasn't enough for the strange bear? What if he came after *her* next? As they raced up the slope, Kallik glanced back and saw that the bear wasn't chasing them. Instead, he was bent over the dead seal, tearing into it.

"It's not fair!" she wailed. "That was our seal!"

"I know," Nisa said with a sigh. Her paws seemed heavy as she slowed down to a walk.

"Why should that lazy bear get our meal, when you did all the work of catching it?" Kallik insisted.

"That bear needs to eat as much as we do," Nisa said. "When seals are scarce, you have to get used to fighting for every meal. You can't trust any other bears, my cubs. We must stick together, because we are the only ones who will look after one another."

Kallik and Taqqiq exchanged glances. Kallik knew she would do anything to take care of her mother and her brother. She hadn't seen many other bears, but when she had, they had been big and fierce and scary, just like the one that had stolen their seal. Maybe white bears weren't meant to have friends. Maybe the ice didn't allow it.

"We'll be all right if we stay together," Nisa promised. "There's food to be found if you know where to look, and if you're patient enough to catch it. So don't get your head all matted with snow about it. I'll be here to look after you until you're strong enough to hunt on your own."

She swung her head around to the left. "Can you smell that?"

Kallik sniffed. She did smell something! But it wasn't seal . . . it was something else. Something fishier, but not exactly fish. She didn't recognize it.

"What do you think it is?" she asked Taqqiq. He was crouched down as if he was stalking something, and as she spoke, he leaped forward, pinning down a snowflake that had drifted to the ground. Kallik looked up and saw that it was snowing again. Her brother was happily batting at the snowflakes. It didn't look as if he'd even tried to sniff for what her mother had scented.

"Taqqiq, pay attention," Kallik said. "You'll have to hunt for yourself one day, too."

"All right, bossy paws," Taqqiq said, twitching his nose dramatically from side to side.

"Come along, quickly," Nisa said. "Try not to make too much noise." They followed their mother across the ice, padding as quietly as possible. The scent didn't seem to be moving away.

"Is it staying still?" Kallik asked. "Does that mean it doesn't know we're coming?"

"One way to throw off your prey is to hide your scent," Nisa said. "Like this—follow me." She led them to a channel of melted water in the ice and they swam across one by one.

"Blech, now my fur's all wet," Taqqiq complained, shaking himself as they climbed out the other side.

"That should make it harder to smell us coming," Nisa said.

"And that big, old bear back there won't be able to follow our trail, either, right?" Kallik said.

"Hopefully," Nisa said, touching Kallik's muzzle with hers.

As they got closer, the fishy scent got stronger, and Kallik could smell salt and blood and faraway ocean scents mingled with it. Soon she saw a dark shape lying on the ice. At first she thought it must be a giant seal, from the way the flippers were splayed out, but then she saw that it was the carcass of a whale. Huge chunks had been torn off it, and there were large bite marks and claw slashes in its side. The snow around it was covered in blood.

"It's a gray whale," Nisa explained. "Another bear must have killed it and dragged it onto the ice."

Kallik stared at the carcass in awe. It must have been a very strong bear to overpower something so big and pull it all the way out of the water. Even with the large bites taken out of it, there was still plenty for the three of them to eat. Hungrily, she stretched out her muzzle and tugged a piece of meat free.

Nisa nudged her, making her drop the meat. "Don't forget to express gratitude to the spirits of the ice," Kallik's mother said gently. "You must always remember that you are part of a bigger world." She bowed her head and touched her nose to the ice. "We thank you, spirits of the ice, for guiding us to this meal," she murmured. Kallik imitated her mother, whispering the same words, and Taqqiq followed. Then, with happy rumbles, they began to eat.

The fog had rolled away by the time night fell, and the stars shone brightly in a clear sky. Kallik sprawled on the ice, her full belly keeping her warm. Next to her were her mother and brother. Not a hint of a breeze stirred the fur on their shoulders; for once, the wind had died down and the sea far beneath the ice was silent.

"Mother?" Kallik asked. "Please tell me again about the spirits under the ice."

Taqqiq gave a little huff of laughter, but Nisa touched her nose to her daughter's side with a serious expression.

"When a white bear dies," she said, "its spirit sinks into the ice, lower and lower, until all you can see is a shadow under the ice. But you shouldn't be frightened of them, little star. The spirits are there to guide you. If you are a good bear, they will always be there to take care of you and help you find food or shelter."

"I'd rather *you* took care of me," Kallik said with a shiver.

"I'll take care of you, too," her mother promised.

"What about the ice spots in the sky?" Kallik said, pointing her muzzle upward. "Aren't those the spirits of bears, too?"

"When the ice melts," Nisa explained, "the bear spirits escape and drift up to the sky on the snow-winds, light as snowflakes, where they become stars. Those spirits are watching you, too, only from farther away."

"What about that star over there?" Taqqiq asked. "The one that's really bright. I've even seen it in the daytime, once, and it never moves like the others do."

"That's the Pathway Star," Nisa said.

"Why is it called the Pathway Star?" Taqqiq prompted.

"Because if you follow it," Nisa said solemnly, "it will lead you to a place far, far away where the ice never melts."

"Never?" Kallik gasped. "You mean there's no burn-sky? We could hunt all the time?"

"No burn-sky, no melting ice, no eating berries or living on the land," Nisa said. "The bear spirits dance for joy across the sky, all in different colors."

"Why don't we go there?" Taqqiq asked. "If it's so wonderful?" Kallik nodded. She felt a tingling in her paws, as if she could run all the way to this place where they would be safe forever.

"It is a long way away," Nisa rumbled. "Much too far for us to travel." Her black eyes stared into the distance, silvery glints of the moon swimming in their depths. "But perhaps we may have to make the journey . . . one day."

"Really? When?" Kallik demanded, but her mother rested her head on her paws and fell silent. She obviously didn't want to answer any more questions. Kallik curled into a ball in the curve of her mother's side and watched the ice shimmering under the moon until she fell asleep. In her dreams, bear spirits rose from the ice and began to dance, their paws light as fur as they romped and slid across the frozen landscape.

A strange creaking noise woke Kallik the next morning. It sounded like a bear yawning loudly, or the wind howling from underwater, but the air was still, and the noise came from the ice, not the sky. Her mother was already awake, padding in a circle around them with her nose lifted.

Kallik scrambled to her paws and shook herself. Her coat felt heavy with moisture, and the air was damp and soft instead of crisp and clear like it had been the night before. She turned to her brother, who was lying on the ice beside her, apparently still asleep. She nudged him with her muzzle.

"Walrus attack!" Taqqiq bellowed, suddenly leaping to his paws and knocking her over. Nisa spun around with a snarl, but stopped when she saw that her cubs were just playing.

"Quiet," she growled. "Taqqiq, stop acting like a wild goose. There is no time for playing. We have to get moving." She started across the ice without looking back. Kallik and Taqqiq scrambled to catch up. Nisa's grouchiness made Kallik nervous. Why would she scold them for playing now, when she'd let them roll around having fun the day before?

The creaking began again as they traveled across the ice. Nisa paused and swung her head around to listen. It seemed like the sound of the ice groaning and yawning underpaw was getting louder. Kallik could tell that her mother knew what this sound was—and that it meant something very bad.

Suddenly there was a loud crack and a horrible sucking noise, and Kallik felt the ground tilt below her. She was thrown off her paws and found herself sliding along ice that was no longer flat but sloped down steeply toward dark water. With a terrified squeal, Kallik scrabbled on the ice, her claws sliding helplessly on the slick surface.

A giant paw grabbed her and hauled her backward onto solid ice again. Kallik stumbled as Nisa bundled her away from the crack in the ice, where waves slapped hungrily against the new edge.

"Wow!" Taqqiq yelped. "The ice just snapped in two! Kallik, I thought you'd be swallowed up by the sea and we'd never see you again!"

Nisa hissed with frustration. Kallik peered around her mother's legs and saw that the ice in front of them had broken into two large chunks that were drifting apart on the sea.

"Already?" Nisa muttered. "But we've had no time at all on the ice! How are we supposed to survive on land if we can't hunt for long enough before?" She paced along the jagged edge of the ice, snarling at the waves that lapped at her paws.

"Mother?" Kallik whimpered. "What's happening? Is it . . . is it burn-sky?"

"It's too early for burn-sky," Nisa said. "But the ice-melt is coming earlier each season. We have less and less time to hunt." She chuffed angrily. "It can't go on like this."

"What do we do?" Kallik asked. "What's going to happen to us if the ice melts too soon?"

Nisa just growled, pawing the edge of the ice.

"Should we move to land?" Taqqiq asked. "Isn't that what we're supposed to do when the ice melts?"

"No," Nisa said, lifting her muzzle. "We must continue to hunt, or else we shall not survive the long, hungry months of burn-sky."

"But—" Kallik started, glancing at the surging water and broken ice before them. What if the ice all melted before they could get to the land?

"We must go on," Nisa insisted. "We cannot go to the land yet—or we will all die."

She moved off across the ice, and Taqqiq followed her. Kallik paused for a moment on the jagged edge, the dark water lapping at her paws. She stared at the broken chunk of ice floating across the water from her. How far was it to land? Was there enough ice left for them to get there? And if there wasn't . . . what would happen to them?

SEEKERS

Also by ERIN HUNTER

WARRIORS

THE NEW PROPHECY